BACK IN BUSINESS

Babies Versus Kittens

Adapted by Patty Michaels

Ready-to-Read

Simon Spotlight
New York   London   Toronto   Sydney   New Delhi

SIMON SPOTLIGHT
An imprint of Simon & Schuster Children's Publishing Division
1230 Avenue of the Americas, New York, New York 10020
This Simon Spotlight edition August 2019
DreamWorks The Boss Baby Back in Business © 2019 DreamWorks Animation LLC.
All Rights Reserved, including the right of reproduction in whole or in part in any form.
SIMON SPOTLIGHT, READY-TO-READ, and colophon are registered trademarks of
Simon & Schuster, Inc.
For information about special discounts for bulk purchases, please contact
Simon & Schuster Special Sales at 1-866-506-1949 or business@simonandschuster.com.
Manufactured in the United States of America 0719 LAK
10 9 8 7 6 5 4 3 2 1
ISBN 978-1-5344-5069-1 (hc)
ISBN 978-1-5344-5068-4 (pb)
ISBN 978-1-5344-5070-7 (eBook)

Bootsy Calico was thrilled.
Today he would finally
defeat Boss Baby!

It was time to take

over the town!

The first part of his plan was to distract the mayor.

Then Bootsy called

Boss Baby.

Bootsy told him
that six kittens
would be causing
trouble all over town.

Boss Baby could not
leave his room.

His friends came over
to help him.

"Bootsy Calico has got six kittens trying to hurt the town!" Boss Baby said.

"We will work together
to stop them!"

Bootsy sent
a map of where
to find the kittens.

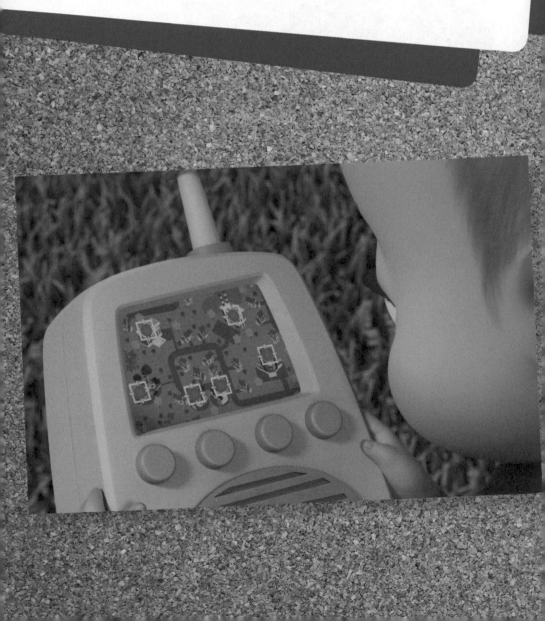

"He is daring us to
stop them in time,"
Boss Baby said.

Boss Baby was too late.

A kitten jumped on

a reporter!

Another kitten pretended
to be stuck in a tree.

Police and firefighters
came to help.

One kitten scared people
by meowing like an alarm.

One of the triplets tried
to catch a naughty kitten.
It did not work.

The kittens were

causing trouble.

The people and the town were in danger!

The plan was working.

"No more love for anyone!"

Bootsy shouted.

The babies needed a plan!

Just then Tim arrived.
He and Boss Baby
came up with an idea.

The idea was to pretend
that a baby needed help.
They safely strapped
the baby to a branch.

They hoped it would bring the town back together.

People came to help.

Everyone stopped fighting!

Now it was time
to stop Bootsy.

Bootsy was no match
for all the babies!